Amanda Bean's Amazing Dream

For my heavenly Father and my family: Bruce, Tim, and Seth — C.N.

For my family, especially Tom — L.W.

Library of Congress Cataloging-in-Publication Data

Neuschwander, Cindy
Amanda Bean's amazing dream: a mathematical story /
story by Cindy Neuschwander; pictures by Liza Woodruff;
math activities by Marilyn Burns.
p. cm.
"A Marilyn Burns brainy day book."
Summary: Amanda loves to count everything, but not until she has
an amazing dream does she finally realize that being able to multiply will
help her count things faster.
ISBN 978-0-590-30012-4
[1. Multiplication—Fiction. 2. Arithmetic—Fiction. 3. Dreams—Fiction.
4. Schools—Fiction.]
I. Woodruff, Liza, ill. II. Burns, Marilyn III. Title.
PZ7.N4453Am 1998
[E]—dc21 97-7056
CIP
AC

30 29 28 27 26 25 24 23 13 14 15 16/0

Printed in Malaysia 108
First edition, August 1998

The display face is Snap ITC.
The text face is Leawood Book.
The art is pen and ink and watercolor.

Amanda Bean's Amazing Dream

A Mathematical Story

Story by **Cindy Neuschwander**

Pictures by **Liza Woodruff**

Math Activities by **Marilyn Burns**

SCHOLASTIC PRESS • NEW YORK

A Marilyn Burns Brainy Day Book

I am Amanda Bean and I love math. I know all about counting. I am very good at it. I can count by ones, twos, fives, and tens. I can add up anything. The kids at school call me Bean Counter.

"Hey! What are you counting, Bean Counter?" they yell.

"Anything and everything!" I yell back. "I just like to know how many."

I count every day, even when I am on my way home from school.

Now we are learning about multiplying. I understand many things about multiplying. I know that it is like adding lots of things quickly.

This is good.

I know about the multiplication sign, ×. It means that things can come in groups, or rows, or columns.

This is also good.

What I do not know are the multiplication facts. My teacher says it is important to learn these. I am not so sure. I think I can just keep counting. I tell my teacher this. He agrees, but he says counting is a longer way to find the same answer.

I think about this when I get home. I think about this as I eat a snack in our kitchen. I look at the tile countertop.

"The *countertop*," I say. "I must count these tiles."

I notice there are 12 columns of tiles. There are 12 tiles in each column. It is a long time before I count all 144 of them. I am Amanda Bean and I like to work quickly. Maybe multiplying would be faster.

I walk to the library to check out a book. One bookcase has seven shelves and nine books on each shelf. I am Amanda Bean and I count anything and everything.

I start counting.

I finally figure out that there are 63 books in the bookcase. I am happy to know this, but now the library is closing. It is too late for me to look for a book. Maybe I should learn to multiply. Maybe it would make counting easier.

I am still thinking about this when I go to bed. I am very tired, but my mind just will not quit thinking about numbers. Once, when I could not sleep, my mother told me to count sheep. I stayed awake all night counting them. The next morning I had 6,727 sheep in my head. I do not think counting sheep is for me.

Tonight I will think about riding my bike. This is simple. There are only two wheels, two pedals, one seat, and one of me.

"I will imagine a quiet ride in the country," I whisper to myself. I can see the rolling hills, the big trees, and the green grass.

"This is relaxing," I say as I begin to nod off.

I am pedaling along a quiet back road. The sun is shining. A gentle breeze is brushing against my face. This *is* relaxing!

Then I notice something. It looks like eight bicycles with sheep on them.

"How many wheels is that?" I wonder. I start counting, but the sheep whiz by so fast, I cannot count all the bicycle wheels.

"Wait!" I yell. "I am Amanda Bean and I count anything and everything!"

I decide to follow them. I have to know how many wheels have rolled by me. Then I wonder, "How many legs do those sheep have altogether?"

Now I really must catch up with those woolies on wheels. I really must know how many. I pump harder. I breathe harder. Up the hill they go. Up the hill I go. Around the bend they go. Around the bend I go.

The sheep stop at a barn and get off their bikes. I get off my bike, too. I do not stop to count the wheels. I follow the sheep. They go into the barn. I go in, too. They reach into their fleecy pockets. Each sheep pulls out five balls of beautiful yarn.

"Oh, no!" I cry out. "Now I must count the yarn, too! I am Amanda Bean and I count anything and everything. First it was wheels. Then it was legs. Now it's balls of yarn!"

I cannot believe my eyes at what I see next. Seven grandmas come marching in with two knitting needles each. They take the yarn from the sheep and start knitting sweaters.

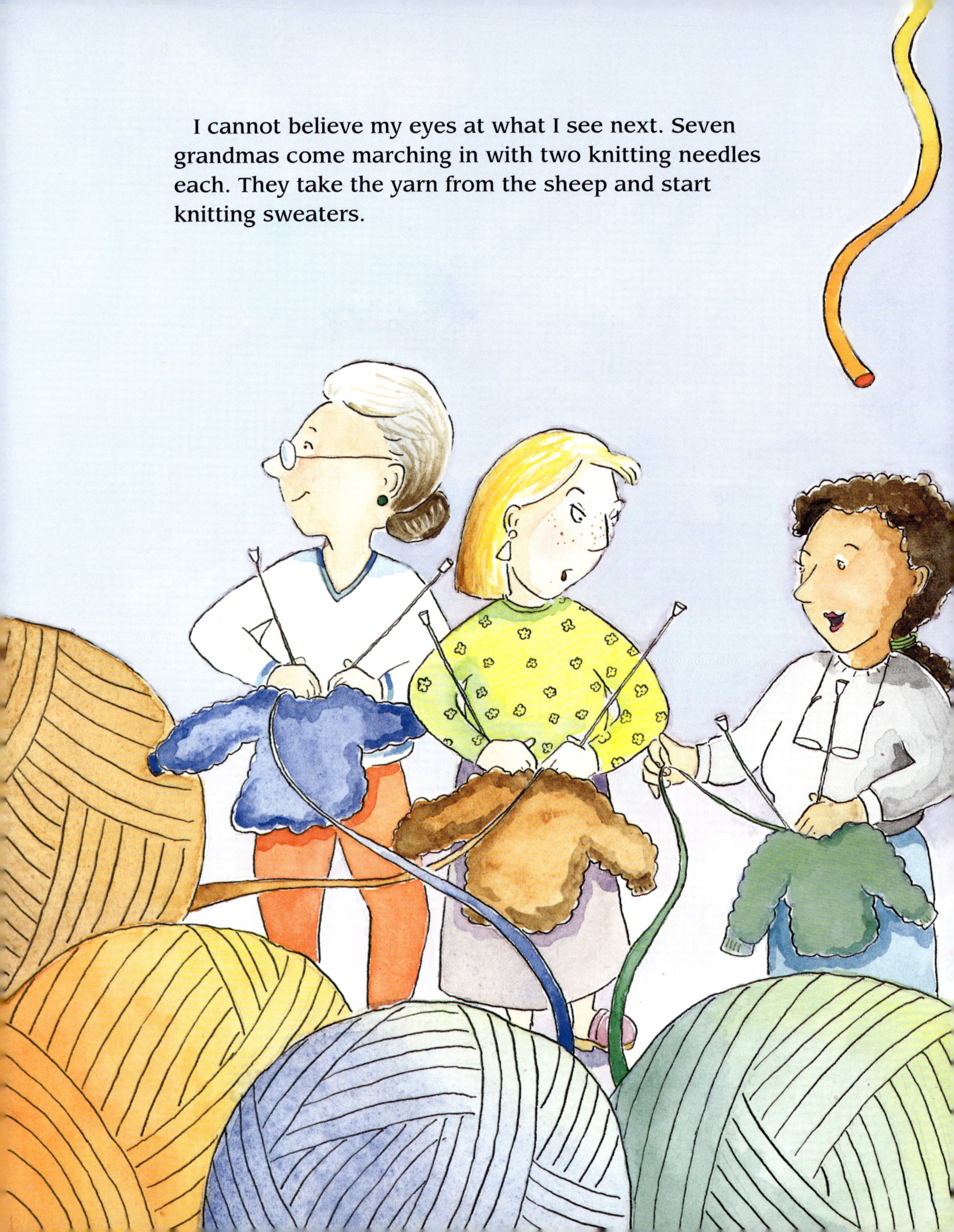

This dream is getting too crazy! Now I must add knitting needles to my list of things to count. And each sweater has two arms. Should I count them, too?

The grandmas start wrapping all of the sweaters around me.
"Stop!" I tell them. "How can I count all of the arms in the sweaters, and all of the knitting needles, and the balls of yarn, and the sheep's legs, and the bicycle wheels if I am all wrapped up?"

"M-u-l-t-i-p-l-y," bleat the sheep.

"Multiply! Multiply! Multiply!" chant the grandmas.

"Multiply?" I ask. "I am Amanda Bean and I count anything and everything," I say.

"Multiplying *is* counting," say the grandmas. "It is just a fast way of counting."

"Y-a-a-h-h-h," agree the sheep.

I wake up to find my mother wrapping me in her arms.

"I had an amazing dream," I say.

"It was a noisy dream," my mother says.

"Today I will start to learn the multiplication facts," I announce. "They are important to know if you want to find out how many . . . and you need to know fast."

My mother agrees.

I am Amanda Bean. I still love knowing how many, but now I *multiply* anything and everything.

And I never count sheep!

For Parents, Teachers, and Other Adults
by Marilyn Burns

When asked what they remember about learning multiplication in elementary school, most adults will answer: memorizing times tables. Only a few, however, recall being taught *why* multiplication is useful and *how* it relates to the world around us. By showing examples of multiplication in different contexts, *Amanda Bean's Amazing Dream* helps children understand what multiplication is and gives them a compelling reason for learning to use this basic operation of arithmetic.

About the Mathematics

When learning about multiplication, it's important for children to think about multiplication in two ways—numerically as repeated addition of the same quantities, and geometrically as rows and columns in rectangular arrays. The illustrations in *Amanda Bean's Amazing Dream* provide many examples to support children's learning. The groups of lollipops, wheels on bicycles, balls of yarn, and pairs of knitting needles give children a numerical view, while the windows and panes, tiles on a counter, and arrangements of baked goods on trays connect multiplication and geometry. And all of the examples in the story help children see how multiplication relates to the world around them.

Extending Children's Learning

1. After reading the story, revisit each illustration and talk with your child about different ways to count the objects.

For example, look at the building farthest to the left in the illustration at the beginning of the story. There are six large windows, each divided into smaller panes. Ask your child how many panes there are in one of the windows. Your child may count the panes one by one, or figure in some other way. In either case, to check the answer and help your child see other ways to solve the problem, offer an alternative. You may say, "There are six rows with three panes in each, so I can add 3 six times, once for each row—3, 6, 9, 12, 15, 18." Or, "The window has three columns with six panes in each, so I can add three 6s—6, 12, 18." Or, "The window is shaped like a rectangle that's three panes across and six panes down. I know there are 18 panes because 3 times 6 is 18."

Keep in mind that although it's important for children to learn the multiplication facts, the goal of figuring the number of window panes is not to have children memorize that 6 times 3 is 18. Rather, it is for your child to see how multiplication relates to addition and connects to a problem. Memorization is an eventual goal that should follow, not lead, building understanding of the concept.

Continue with other examples of multiplication on that same beginning illustration with these questions:

How many windows are there on the second building from the left? How many window panes in each? How many window panes altogether in that building?

How many cookies are on each tray in the bakery window? How many in all?

How many lollipops are stuck in each block? How many lollipops are there altogether?

Continue through the book, next looking at the illustration of inside the bakery:

How many brownies or cookies are on the bakery shelves?

How many cakes are in the display cabinet?

How many stripes are there on all the loaves of bread?

What other problems like these could you solve in the bakery?

Amanda climbs a tree in the park across the street:

How many flowers are in the rectangle in the center of the park?

How many flowers are in the border?

Amanda continues counting when she's in the kitchen at home:

How many tiles are on the counter?

How many mugs are in the cabinet?

How many kernels of popcorn was Amanda pouring into the bowl? (In this example, the popcorn isn't organized in any particular way that makes multiplication useful. Talk with your child about how you might organize the popcorn kernels by 2s, 5s, and other ways.)

When Amanda's dream gets underway, there are more problems to solve:

How many wheels are there on eight bicycles?

How many legs are there on eight sheep?

If each sheep has five balls of yarn, how many balls of yarn do they have altogether?

How many knitting needles do the seven grandmas have?

How many arms are there altogether in the sweaters the grandmas knitted?

If your child isn't interested in answering all of these problems in one sitting, don't push beyond his or her interest level. Try several, letting your child choose. Revisiting the book later gives further opportunities for more thinking.

2. Play "Things that Come in Groups" with your child. For example, ask your child, "What things come in 2s?" Brainstorm ideas—wheels on bicycles, shoes in a pair, birds' wings, people's eyes, slices of bread in a sandwich; and so on. Then ask your child to think about things that come in groups for other numbers. Emphasize that the things must come in the *same size* groups—soft drinks in six-packs, eggs in cartons, tentacles on octopuses, wheels on tricycles, wings on butterflies, and so on. Real-world examples emphasize the usefulness of multiplication for figuring out how many there are when things are organized into groups: *How many eggs are there in three cartons? How many wheels on eight tricycles?*

To help your child become comfortable with multiples, practice counting by 2s, 5s, and 10s. Then move to 3s, 4s, 6s, and other numbers. It's often easier for children to learn to count by multiples when they can relate the numbers to real-world contexts. For example, if your child is familiar with football, counting by 7s may be easier if he or she thinks about touchdowns.

3. Play "Which Has More?" to help your child figure and compare answers to multiplication problems.

Which has more panes—a window with 5 rows and 4 panes in each row or a window with 3 rows and 6 panes in each?

Which has more cookies—3 rows with 8 cookies in each row or 4 rows with 6 cookies in each?

Which has more wheels—5 tricycles or 7 bicycles?

Have paper and pencil available in case your child wants to make numerical notes or drawings. Have fun with your child making up other problems like these.